DATE DUE

ANNA GROSSNICKLE HINES

Miss Emma's Wild Garden

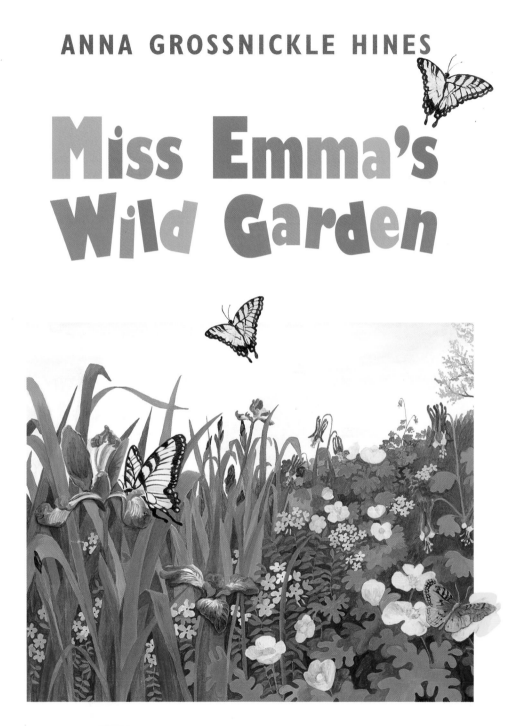

 Greenwillow Books, New York

"Your garden is wild, Miss Emma, not all in rows like my papa's," Chloe said.

"I like it wild," said Miss Emma. "I like to let things grow any crazy way they want."

"Wild and crazy," Chloe agreed. "I like to grow that way, too. What's in your garden, Miss Emma?"

"Oh, my! Lots of things: shooting stars, foam flowers, wild blue phlox, and bleeding hearts."

"And violets and bluebells and dandelions," Chloe added. "My papa doesn't like dandelions, but I do."

Miss Emma nodded. "So do I, child. They're like little golden sunshines."

"What else, Miss Emma? Do you have wild creatures in your garden?"

"Indeed I do! I have deer that eat the flower buds,
and rabbits nibbling the wild ginger."
"What else do you have?"

"A woodchuck and her baby come to eat the sweet cicely and violets," Miss Emma said. "They're hungry rascals."

"I like the baby one. Can I pet it?" Chloe asked.

"No, no. It's too wild."

"Too bad. What else do you have in your garden?"

"Well, let's see. There's a cardinal nesting in the forsythia
bush," Miss Emma said. "Don't disturb her now."
"I won't," Chloe promised. "The papa cardinal is kissing her."
"He's giving her seeds to eat," said Miss Emma.
"I like that," Chloe said. "He's a nice papa cardinal. What
else is in your garden?"

"Here's a skink sunning on a rock, a young one
with a bright blue tail."
"Blue like my shirt," said Chloe. "What else,
Miss Emma?"

"There's a nuthatch on the trunk of that maple tree, and up higher a squirrel is scolding. See? They're upside down."

"No, they aren't," Chloe said. "They're the same as me. You're the upside-down one, Miss Emma. What else is in your garden?"

"Oh, a toad hides in the forget-me-nots
beside the creek, and lots of earthworms
live in the soil. They eat all the rotting
leaves."
"And what else?"

"Butterflies and bees sip the nectar
from the blossoms."
"And what else?"

"What else, child? You make me tired with your what elses," Miss Emma said. "I don't know what else."

"But there's one more thing," Chloe said. "One more wild creature in your garden."

"Then suppose you tell me," Miss Emma said. "You just tell me what else is in my garden."

"Me!" Chloe said. "I'm in your garden."

"Indeed you are, child," Miss Emma agreed. "You are the best wild creature in my wild, crazy garden."

For Grandma,
whose wonderful garden grew in rows

Acrylic paint was used for the full-color art.
The text type is Rotis Sans Serif.

Printed in Hong Kong by South China Printing Company (1988) Ltd.
First Edition 10 9 8 7 6 5 4 3 2 1

Library of Congress Cataloging-in-Publication Data

Hines, Anna Grossnickle.
Miss Emma's wild garden / by Anna Grossnickle Hines.
　　　p.　　cm.
Summary: A young girl asks about all the wild creatures that
can be found in her older friend's garden, from rabbits and
woodchucks to butterflies and bees—and one very exuberant child.
ISBN 0-688-14692-9 (trade).　　ISBN 0-688-14693-7 (lib. bdg.)
[1. Gardens—Fiction.　　2. Animals—Fiction.]　　I. Title
PZ7.H572Mi　　1997　　[E]—dc20
96-6291　　CIP　　AC